How Good Are Your Love Instincts?

Your husband tells you he needs to find closure with the high school sweetheart who dumped him. Your best option is:

a) Seduce him and make him forget all about her
b) Ask him to define "closure"
c) Send him to a psychiatrist
d) Help him search the Internet for her

You make the colossal mistake of choosing answer D on the previous question, and your husband leaves you for his high school sweetheart. You should:

a) Get a makeover
b) Follow your almost ex-husband to his new town (to show him what he threw away when he left you)
c) Romance the local serial killer (because you really don't believe he's a serial killer even though he does bring home lots of large plastic containers and bury wrapped bundles in his backyard)
d) All of the above

Bobbie's final answer was definitely D—she was in big trouble!

Dear Reader,

I believe the best thing about writing is getting to ask the "what if" question. Possibilities abound, and one of those possibilities gave birth to *Sex and the Serial Killer*. What if you thought you were doing everything right in your marriage and suddenly found that you'd done everything absolutely wrong? That "what if" begins Bobbie Jones's journey. When her husband, Warren, calls from amidst the rumpled sheets of his lover's bed to ask for a divorce, Bobbie's life turns upside down and inside out. She quits her job, gets a new haircut and a new look, then follows Warren to Cottonmouth, California, where she'll show him what a big mistake he's made. And she'll flaunt a new man in his face. Sexy as the devil himself, Nick Angel is the perfect candidate for flaunting. Except that everyone in Cottonmouth thinks Nick's a serial killer.

Bobbie will touch the sky and hit rock bottom before she finally finds everything she's looking for in Cottonmouth. I had a wonderful time exploring Bobbie's "what if." She made me laugh and made me cry, as did the people she met on her journey.

Enjoy!

Jennifer Skullestad

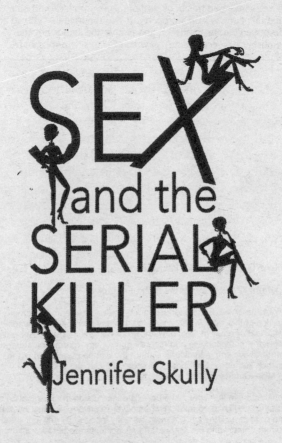

SEX and the SERIAL KILLER

Jennifer Skully

HQN™

ISBN 0-373-77027-8

SEX AND THE SERIAL KILLER

Copyright © 2005 by Jennifer Skullestad

www.HQNBooks.com

Printed in U.S.A.